A Cornish folk tale

MERYON

told by Gill Peters
illustrated by Barbara Peters

Book design by Michael Bradley

PYLLEN BOOKS

First Edition 2010

Copyright © Gillian Peters
Illustrations copyright © Barbara Peters

ISBN 978-0-9565795-0-8

Published by Pyllen Books
10, Kings's Avenue,
Falmouth TR11 2QH

Printed by R. Booth Ltd.
12 The Praze,
Penryn.
Cornwall.

Rael ger
gans cowethas,
'rag Julie x Helston Class!

Yth yw an lyver ma rag agan flehes

Gill Peters

Barbara Peters

Dec 2010.

When the mist rolls in from the sea it covers the roads, the rocks and the wind-bent trees in the far west of Cornwall.

Sometimes the rain comes damping down, or pours like water from a bucket. In dark days like these, people used to think that piskies came and led them astray. When they missed their path or fell, they were sure that they were pisky-led.

But on fine days the sky is blue, the sea waves dance and sparkle and the gorse buds pop in the sun.

This is a magic land. Here, a long time ago, Tom Treva lived by the village of Morvah.

Tom and his wife had four great boys who worked in the mine and on the land. Their youngest child was a girl. They called her "our little Meryon" because she was as busy as an ant. (Meryon is an old word for ant."

The family were poor. Meryon had her granny's old dresses cut down to fit her. She wore them until they were full of patches, and the other girls laughed at her. Then the brothers would comfort her by saying, "next Feast Tide we will have saved enough to buy a new dress." But there never was money to spare.

In spite of this Meryon was always happy. Her parents were loving and her brothers were kind. She had hair the colour of a blackbird's wing and eyes of forget-me-not blue. She sang as she worked in the house and garden.

On sunny days she walked in the country gathering berries and wild flowers. She would lie in the meadow grass and watch the clouds floating like tufts of lamb's wool across the sky. One day she found a four-leaved clover and she wished for......Oh! But wishes are secret or they won't come true.

Then cousin Morwenna came to visit.

She had gone into service with a family in town. Now she had

come back wearing fine clothes.

She jangled her bracelets and twirled her necklace round her

fingers.

She said, "If you had a proper dress, Meryon, I would take you to

Morvah Fair.

But I won't be seen with you in those rorey-torey clothes. You look

like an owl in an ivy bush. Leave home. Go and find work and then

you can dress like me. Daisy chain bracelets and flower crowns are

only for children and not for girls like us."

After Cousin Morwenna left, Meryon begged her father to let her

go into the world and find her fortune. At first Tom Treva said "No."

No one in the family wanted her to leave.

Then he said, " Maybe some day, my bird."

Meryon pleaded with him so often that in the end he agreed.

"You may go at the start of the year when the weather is fine," he

said.

On the first day of spring she was ready. Her father said, "Go no

further than three day's length from home. Come back if you are

unhappy. Until we see you again take care and work hard. Send

word if you need us. Good-bye, my dear child."

To hide her tears Meryon bent down and stroked the little cat that

purred around her ankles. Then she took up her bundle and pasty

and set off.

At the top of the fields above the village she turned for one last look at her home. She felt a little afraid. What would she find in the wide world? Would she be safe on her journey? She said under her breath.

 "Don't you come to frighten me, bad Bucca-dhu." Then she laughed at her fears and walked on. The day was clear and the sun was warm on her back.

At noonday she stopped at a well by the wayside to eat her pasty. When she had finished she unlaced her boots to rest her feet. She washed her face and dried it on her apron.

Looking down into the water she said

  "By hedge and stile and hawthorn tree,

   Send good fortune soon for me."

A voice came back to her,

  "By hill and stream and wishing well,

   I am here with news to tell."

As she peered into the well in astonishment she heard laughter. She turned with a start and saw a handsome gentleman holding a little boy by the hand.

" Good day to you," he said. " You are wishing for good fortune. Where are you going to find it?"

"Oh sir, I am just on my way to look for work, " said Meryon.

"Then truly it is lucky for us both that we met here on the road. I need somebody to care for my little boy and my house. You have a kind face. Come with us." Meryon looked at them both. The little boy looked at her unblinking. The man smiled and pointed at her feet. All fingers and thumbs, Meryon put on her boots and did up the laces. She stood up and said," If you will pay me I have a mind to go with you. I can bake and sew and clean. I can plant and weed the garden. But I have never looked after a child before."

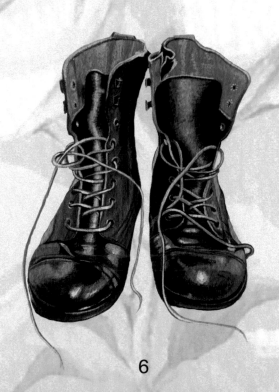

"You will find it an easy task, I promise you," said the man. "My name is Cador and this is Robin, my son. Now, my little Robin, how will you like it if Meryon looks after you?"

 "I can't tell yet," said little Robin.

Cador laughed. Meryon wondered how he knew her name, but she dared not ask. She saw that both man and child looked pleasant but strange. They had dark eyes and faces the colour of walnut skins. Their ears were curiously shaped.

 "We should be on our way. It is a long mile to our home and we must get there before the sun goes down," said Cador.

Robin put his hand in Meryon's They walked up and down and roundabout, in lanes and byways without stopping. They ate cakes, shivery sweet to the taste, from Cador's basket, and drank wild herb cordial as they went. Meryon listened to Robin's chatter, putting one foot in front of the other and not watching where she was going. Then suddenly she breathed in a wonderful perfume. Looking to left and to right she saw trees and flowers that she had never seen before.

She felt she had woken up into a dream as she walked between hedges of bright leaf and blossom.

At sunset they came to a wood. A small stream ran in front of them. Walking on soft green moss to the edge, they crossed by the stepping -stones. Through a gate ahead Meryon could see a house half hidden among the trees. A twisting path led to an open door.

"We are home, Dadda," said little Robin, smiling.

He ran through the gate to the garden where rabbits played on the grass and birds scratched for worms. To Meryon's surprise they were not startled and did not hide.

"How beautiful this is!" she exclaimed, stretching out her arms as if she wanted to hold all she could see.

"Welcome to our home," said Cador as they followed Robin to the door. Meryon stepped over the threshold into a room full of evening shadows. A large pot hung over the hearth fire and in the far corner sat an old woman in a rocking chair.

She was bundled up in many clothes. Meryon could see a creased face under the frills of a large bonnet. Robin was leaning against her knee and she had a leathery hand on his shoulder.

"This is Mother Cronack, " he said to Meryon. "She watches over us."

The old woman leaned forward and said in a croaky voice

" I will watch you at home

Or wherever you roam.

In this place you will stay

And never must stray."

Meryon did not know what to say to that so she bobbed a curtsy.

Mother Cronack nodded her head and set the chair rocking.

"Now Mother Cronack," said Cador, "we shall see what you have in the pot for our meal." He fetched bowls and ladled soup into them. He brought bread from the cupboard to the table and said, "Sit you down and we will eat."

After the soup they ate strange fruits and drank milk as cold as well water and scented with jasmine flowers. Meryon forgot her home, her mother and father and her brothers.

" Now I will tell you what you must do," said Cador. "Rise with the sun in the morning. Clean the house and work in the garden. Then give little Robin flowery milk and take him to the stream. Put these drops on his eyelids. Always remember they are only for him. You may walk with him and let him play in the orchard, but never go into the wood. There is danger."

Meryon promised that she would do as he said.

Every day Cador rode away on a fine horse. Then Meryon worked in the house and garden. She and Robin fed the chickens and collected the eggs. They petted the rabbits, weeded the flowerbeds and played games. Every day was fine. When Meryon put the drops on Robin's eyes he laughed and clapped his hands and danced like a wild one.

Sometimes she would jump across the stepping-stones and look into the wood, but it seemed dark and whispery so she was not tempted to go in. At the end of the day she would wash little Robin in the stream and they would go home in time to greet Cador as he rode up to the door.

But every day Meryon wondered what would happen if she tried the drops herself. One day while Robin played she took the bottle and looked at it.

Then she opened it and shook some drops on her eyelids. It stung so she splashed water from the stream on her face. When her eyes had cleared, she turned round and saw Robin playing with a crowd of small people in the orchard. They were climbing trees, hide and seeking, skipping, running and even flying. Meryon sat and watched enchanted while the time ran away. When Mother Cronack came from the house to call them for supper, Meryon could see quite clearly that she was a toad.

Robin came and said, "Time to go home to Dadda." She washed him in the stream, cleaned her own face and they went back to the house.

Meryon looked sideways at Mother Cronack who spoke to her in her croaky old voice.

" A toad watches well,

But a toad doesn't tell."

She patted Meryon's hand kindly.

Once she had tried the magic drops Meryon could not stop herself from using them again. She became bolder. Seeing that Mother Cronack was watching Robin, she crossed the stream and walked into the wood. No birds sang and under the trees all was silent. She crept along until she could see a clearing ahead. There were voices and laughter and as she went nearer she could see a crowd of brightly dressed gentlemen on horseback. In the centre was Cador. A horn sounded and they wheeled their horses and galloped away.

Curious to learn more, and see what they hunted, Meryon went into the wood the next day. She found her way back to the clearing and could hear voices. As she peeped round a tree a hand came over her mouth. She pulled it away and whirled round to see a squat creature with a whiskery face and bared teeth.

"Come with me, my pretty," it said hoarsely.

"Go away, Bucca-dhu " she hissed, "or the fairies will curse you."

The creature grinned all over its ugly face and pulled hard at her arm. Meryon screamed and at that moment there was a crashing sound as Cador rode towards them. The creature turned and fled before him into the trees. The ladies and gentlmen vanished as if into air.

 Meryon stood trembling until Cador returned. Looking down at her with stony eyes he said, " Disobedient girl! You were told not to come into the wood. I banish you from my home."

Meryon wept and begged to be forgiven. After a while he said coldly, "Very well. I will give you a second chance. Do not stray again."

She gave her promise gladly, for she had been very frightened.

The next day when she tried to put the drops in Robin's eyes her hand shook so much that the bottle slipped between her fingers and fell to the ground. In horror Meryon saw her second chance draining away into the grass at her feet.

That day seemed long, and Robin was so cross he told Cador what she had done the minute he rode up to the door.

"I am so sorry," said Meryon, "shall I have to go?"

"No," said Cador with a sigh. "I will have to fetch another bottle in the morning, but it was an accident. You can have a third chance. It is the last. Be very careful."

After that she did not wander off alone, but she still put the drops in her eyes to watch the fairy children at play. Only the toad knew, but a secret is hard to keep, especially from fairy folk.

One evening Cador came home and leaping from his horse he picked Robin up and swung him high above his head. Laughing, he turned to Meryon and said, " How was my little man today?"

"He played happily with all his friends," she said without thinking. Then she put her hand over her mouth and opened her eyes wide when she realised what she had said.

Cador put Robin down and came over to where she stood. He was angry and sad.

"You broke your promise and stole some of the drops, Meryon. You saw all the fairy folk. You have had your last chance. It is finished. Now you must say goodbye to little Robin and leave our home forever."

With tears falling she did as she was bidden, holding the child's hand tightly until she had to let him go. Cador put his hands over her eyes and she fell instantly asleep.

When she woke she was lying by the well where she had met Cador and Robin. The sun was shining down on a bag and bundle by her side. As soon as she saw them she knew that she had not dreamt her adventure. The bundle was full of beautiful clothes, and gold coins were in the small leather bag as payment. Then Meryon understood that she could never go back to that magical world. She said goodbye in her heart to Robin, Cador and old Mother Cronack.

"Well," she said to herself after a while, " I don't belong to sit here moping forever." She picked up her treasures and set out on her journey home.

At the top of the fields above Morvah she started to run towards her house. She was breathless as she ran in through the open door. From the table her parents and her brothers stared with food half way to their mouths. Then suddenly everyone was talking at once. So many questions were asked and she answered none until she said, "How long have I been away?"

"A year and a day, and not a word. We were some worried about you, my Meryon. Where have you been?" asked her father.

"I looked after a little boy for people far away over yonder." She waved her hand vaguely to the distance. "They were good to me. See what I have."

When they saw the money, and had exclaimed over the dresses, she was asked no more. She decided at that moment to keep the secret of little Robin always.

So when Morvah Fair came round again, Meryon could go with the other girls. Her clothes were the envy of Cousin Morwenna who begged her to say how she found such a good place to work.

"Tell me,do. I wish to find work like that."

"Well," said Meryon, smiling secretly, "would you believe me if I said that I was pisky-led?"

"Don't you be so foolish," said Cousin Morwenna. " Nobody would believe that." Meryon laughed and held Morwenna's hand, and so the two girls went down at last to Morvah Fair.

Cornish dialect words:

Bucca-dhu   -   dark or bad spirit

Cronack   -   toad

This story was inspired by the traditional Cornish tale " The Fairy Master"